Oh no! Grumpy Monster is coming for dinner

Written by Ellie Wharton Illustrated by Maxine Lee

Licensed exclusively to Top That Publishing Ltd
Tide Mill Way, Woodbridge, Suffolk, IP12 1AP, UK
www.topthatpublishing.com

2 4 6 8 9 7 5 3 1
Manufactured in China

Written by Ellie Wharton
Illustrated by Maxine Lee

ISBN 978-1-78445-260-5

A catalogue record for this book is available from the British Library

Milly ran down the stairs two at a time. She had seen something rather alarming from her bedroom window and she had to tell Mum as fast as she could.

'Quick, Mum!' she shouted. 'Hide all the china, hang the pots and pans out of reach ... Grumpy Monster is coming to dinner!'

But Mum was as cool as a cucumber and carried on cooking.

Grumpy Monster knocked on the door.

Milly opened the door just a crack, but Grumpy Monster pushed it open and bumbled in.

He tipped the hats off the hat stand, knocked over a vase of flowers and **crashed** into the kitchen.

Milly followed him open-mouthed.

'Do sit down,' said Milly's mum, calmly.

But Grumpy Monster didn't just sit down.
He threw himself down with a thump and broke the chair.

Milly's mum offered him a bigger one.

'Huummmphhh!' frowned Grumpy Monster.

Then, **'Garummmmmppphh!'** he groaned, banging his fists down on the table.

Milly couldn't believe Grumpy Monster's bad manners. But Mum just put a plate of food down gently in front of him ...

... and then another ...

and another ...

and another.

Clever Mum had made all of Grumpy Monster's favourite food!

He guzzled down beans on toast ...

followed by pizza and then a meat and potato dinner ...

... then jelly
and ice cream
for dessert,

all washed down
with a WHOLE jug
of fizzy lemonade!

'BURRRRRRRRRRRRRRRRRPPPPPPP!' went Grumpy Monster.

Mum laughed. Milly laughed.
Grumpy Monster's frown
began to turn upside down ...

He was happy!

And when Grumpy Monster was happy
he did happy things.

He danced the
tango with Mum ...

played hide-and-seek
with Milly ...

and sang karaoke
with them both!

But soon Grumpy Monster was hungry again and his smile began to fade ...

Luckily, clever Mum was always one step ahead.

'Quick!' she said.
'Show him the door, Milly!
I've told him it's time for milk and cookies next door at Tabitha's!'

1

3
1
CRASH
WALLOP
THUD
BANG!